OCTOPUSSY

AGNEATHA

D0435433

MOTLEY

SPIRO

AMON-RA
BLOSSOM

For Enid with love

First published in the United States 1989
by Dial Books
A Division of Penguin Books USA Inc.
375 Hudson Street • New York, New York 10014

Published in Great Britain 1989
by William Collins Sons & Co. Ltd.
 • Printed in Great Britain
1 3 5 7 9 10 8 6 4 2
First Miniature Edition Printing 1992

Library of Congress
Cataloging in Publication Number: 89-1526

Meet My Cats

LESLEY ANNE IVORY

Dial Books  *New York*

Meet My Cats

I have always had cats around me. I got my first kitten, Tissy, when I was five, but did not have another cat until I was married with a little son, James, and we bought Honey. Soon Tickle and Phuan joined us. Now we had three cats, and I had another son, Julian.

Within a very short time three more cats had joined our family: a brown tabby we called Top Cat—TC for short; a beautiful Persian called Ruskin; and a Tabby Point Siamese, Mau-Mau. Then one day on our way home from school I bought Gemma, my first girl.

Gemma

Gemma is a silver, spotted tabby with a white blouse and four socks to match. When her first kittens were ready to be born, she came and called me in from the garden, leading me into the house and the kitchen. There on the kitchen cart she had four kittens. We kept two of them, Muppet and Emu, and found loving homes for the others.

Muppet

Sadly, we lost Emu in a road accident, but Muppet grew into a striking coal-dark tabby. When she was a year old, she gave birth to five kittens in our closet. Of these five we kept one, Gabrielle.

Gabrielle

Gabby is a real chatterbox and never stops chirruping all over the house. She loves chasing and retrieving a ball of paper. She dives after it, and then drops it at your feet for another throw. She cannot stand her granny, Gemma, who hissed at her soon after she was born. Gabby has never forgiven her, and screams every time she meets her.

Twiglet

The coming of Twiglet was a little different. We had originally bought him for the boys' granny, who wanted a little, well-behaved cat. On the way to Granny's, Julian and he became hopelessly attached to each other and were very sad at parting. So both Twiglet and Julian were overjoyed when Granny telephoned the next day to say that after one night of Twiglet she felt she could not cope with him at all! We absorbed him into our family with joy.

Chesterton and Malteazer

Twiglet and Gabby had three kittens, also born in our closet. We called them the Triplikets. Twiglet kept close tracks on his kittens and visited them regularly, helping to wash them at night. Like their mother, they were inveterate talkers and conversations lasted all night. We kept two of them, Chesterton and Malteazer.

Spiro and Blossom

We found Spiro in the local pet shop. He was a soft, pale, honey-ginger.

He grew into a really big cat and was the ringleader with Chesterton and Twiglet in the game of "Raiding." They seemed to know when our neighbors had put bones in their garbage pail, and on a cat-count of one, two, three, off came the lid, and in they went!

Only a few weeks after Spiro came, we were in town and there in a pet shop was Blossom. I bought her at once as a present for Spiro and popped her on top of a bag of oranges.

Blossom and Spiro grew up together and played wonderful rough and tumble games in the garden.

Agneatha

One year we went to Cornwall for a vacation and James stayed behind to look after the cats. When we arrived home, a little fluffy tortoise-shell and white ball blew over the floor to meet us. Agneatha, as James had called her, was a perfect kitten. Her fur grew fluffier and we realized we had a little Persian on our hands. She grew a long white ruff on her chest and posed deliberately and proudly in prominent places, gazing at her reflection in windows.

Agneatha's first litter

Agneatha chose April 1, the day before James's twenty-second birthday, to have her first litter of four kittens, born in a special box with a window cut in it. There was a spotted silver tabby, two little tortoiseshells, and a ginger one. They grew all too soon and the agonizing business of parting with them came around. The ginger one went over the road to friends, so it was not really like seeing him leave home.

Agneatha's second litter

There were five kittens in Agneatha's second litter, of which we kept two. One was a richly marked tabby, Octopussy, so called because he was the eighth kitten born on the eighth day of the eighth month, and the other was little Motley, a dark tortoiseshell.

Amon Ra (Ra-Ra)

Ra Ra was a complete surprise! One Easter, James planned a "different" Easter egg for me—in fact a *Siamese* Chocolate Point Easter egg. Ra Ra is extremely active and mischievous and turns on an amazed, innocent blue stare if one of my precious Greek plates mysteriously "falls" from the dresser, or an egg drops from its basket if he only passes by. He is loving and bites our chins and chews our hair; it is a very good thing for him that we love him too.

And now there are twelve

Twelve really is quite a crowd, and we certainly never planned to have so many, but they are my inspiration, joy, and purpose. I shall always have cats around me.

MUPPET
GEMMA
GABRIELLE
CHESTERTON
TWIGLET
MALTEAZER